W9-AAB-982

The Witch Lady Mystery

Carol Beach York

Illustrated by Ethel Gold

AN
APPLE
PAPERBACK

SCHOLASTIC INC.
New York Toronto London Auckland Sydney

To my beautiful friend
Julie Roche

Scholastic Books are available at special discounts for quantity purchases for use as premiums, promotional items, retail sales through specialty market outlets, etc. For details contact: Special Sales Manager, Scholastic Inc., 730 Broadway, New York, NY 10003, (212) 505-3346.

No part of this publication may be reproduced in whole or in part, or stored in a retrieval system, or transmitted in any form or by any means, electronic, mechanical, photocopying, recording, or otherwise, without written permission of the publisher. For information regarding permission write to Lodestar Books, a division of E.P. Dutton Inc., Two Park Avenue, New York, NY 10016.

ISBN 0-590-40513-6

Copyright © 1976 by Carol Beach York. Illustrations copyright © 1977 by Scholastic Inc. All rights reserved. This edition published by Scholastic Inc., 730 Broadway, New York, NY 10003, by arrangement with Lodestar Books. APPLE PAPERBACKS is a registered trademark of Scholastic Inc.

12 11 10 9 8 7 6 5 4 3 2   6 7 8 9/8 0 1/9

Contents

Exciting News

Oliver was always bringing notices home from school. The notices were printed in pale blue ink and his teacher, Miss Lee, passed them out to the class just before the last bell rang. She would walk along the front of the room and place six notices on the first desk in each row. Oliver, who sat in a front desk, would keep one notice for himself and pass the others to the pupil in the desk behind him. All down the rows the notices would be passed back from desk to desk, while Miss Lee watched with gentle blue eyes to see that no one made too much noise during the procedure.

Usually the notices told what day milk money was

due, or when the next P.T.A. meeting would be held. They were not of much interest to Oliver, but when he got home his mother always read them carefully and nodded her head.

But this afternoon Oliver had a notice of special importance, and he burst into the kitchen with his spelling book and his reader—and the notice.

"What have you got today?" His mother looked up from her ironing. She had brown hair, like Oliver, and long-lashed brown eyes.

Oliver could see that his glass of milk and two graham crackers with peanut butter and jam were already waiting on the kitchen table, but he wanted his mother to read the notice first.

"We're going to have an auction!" Oliver put the notice on the ironing board so his mother could read it right away.

HELP...HELP!
read the top line in bold letters. Down below, the printing was smaller.

Help our school library!
We need new books and more tables and chairs.
Friday afternoon from three to six there will be a
student bake sale and auction.
Please plan to attend!

"A bake sale and auction," Mrs. Woodfield read aloud. She looked up at Oliver. His hair was windblown, and his dark eyes were shining. "Do you know what an auction is?"

Oliver nodded. "Miss Lee told us. We sell things and everybody comes and whoever offers the most money for something gets it."

"That's called 'bidding.'" Oliver's older sister Carrie came in the kitchen door. She was a slender, pretty girl with long brown hair, and she was bristling with importance because she was in the eighth grade and it was the eighth graders who had thought of the idea for the auction.

Carrie set her school books beside Oliver's crumple-cornered spelling book. "Can I bake an angel cake, Mom, and maybe some chocolate-chip cookies for the bake sale?"

"That sounds fine," Mrs. Woodfield said. She ironed the last pillowcase and folded it neatly. "Are you going to take anything for the auction?"

Carrie's glass of milk and graham crackers were next to Oliver's on the table. She sat down and smoothed back her silky hair.

"I'm not exactly going to take something. Some of the kids are going to auction their time, and I'm going to auction two evenings of baby-sitting. So is

Mary Lou." Carrie looked across the table. "How about you, Oliver?"

"Me baby-sit?"

"I didn't mean that." Carrie groaned. "I mean what are you going to *do?*"

Oliver chewed a graham cracker and thought about that. He wasn't sure yet what he could do for the auction.

"A boy in my room is going to offer to wash a hundred windows," Carrie said.

Oliver wrinkled his nose. Washing windows wasn't any fun.

But it did give him an idea.

"I'll rake leaves."

Carrie sipped her milk. "Bob Louis in my room is going to do that too. He's going to offer to keep somebody's yard raked all fall."

Then Carrie began to laugh. "Bob said he hoped Dr. Adams wouldn't win the bidding. There must be a million trees in his yard."

Oliver went to bed that night wondering if somebody with a million trees would bid for him at the auction. That would be a pretty big job. He didn't like raking leaves all *that* much.

The next morning at breakfast he asked his mother

how many trees Dr. Adams really had.

Mrs. Woodfield always looked very pretty at breakfast. She had on rose-colored lipstick and a green robe with a ruffle at the neckline. She was spreading marmalade on her toast, and she looked up when Oliver spoke.

"I don't think anybody around here really has a million trees," she said. "Carrie was exaggerating."

"Okay," Carrie said agreeably. "Dr. Adams probably has only half a million."

Oliver's father stirred cream into his coffee. His eyes twinkled. "If I see Dr. Adams today, shall I tell him to be sure not to miss the auction?"

Carrie grinned. "Think of the good side, Oliver. Maybe the old witch lady will bid for you. She's got only a couple of trees in her backyard, and they're pretty scraggly."

"Boy, are they ever," Oliver agreed.

"Carrie!" Mrs. Woodfield scolded. "I've told you not to call Mrs. Prichard an old witch lady."

Carrie sighed. "Oh, Mom, all the kids call her that."

"Well, they shouldn't," Mrs. Woodfield said firmly.

But we do, Oliver thought. He nudged Carrie's foot under the table. All the kids called Mrs.

Prichard the old witch lady, just as Carrie had said. Mrs. Prichard did weird things—everybody knew that. When she went out she wore a long black coat even on hot summer days, and she walked along the street mumbling to herself and picking twigs from bushes and chewing on them.

Oliver had seen her lots of times, moving along with her slow gait, shrouded in her black coat, chewing the twigs she plucked from the bushes. Light glinted on her spectacles, and an atmosphere of evil seemed to surround her.

And her house was spooky. After dark, when the other houses along the street were bright with light, Mrs. Prichard pulled her blinds down tight, and her windows had only thin streaks of light at the bottom. It was like a ghost house.

In the daytime a huge black cat prowled Mrs. Prichard's yard, and sometimes children on their way to school would see the old witch lady watching from parted curtains. All the kids ran past her house before she could put a bad spell on them.

Oliver thought he would rather rake Dr. Adams' half million trees than take care of the old witch lady's yard.

The Auction

Carrie baked her angel cake and her chocolate-chip cookies. She tied on a big flowery apron and bustled around from cupboard to counter, measuring sugar, sifting flour, beating egg whites. Oliver got to eat a few cookies, but Carrie set aside the rest to take to the bake sale. Oliver tried to sneak a couple more from the plate, but Carrie caught him.

"Oliver, those are for school!" she shrieked.

Oliver thought she had the loudest voice of any girl he had ever heard.

Friday, at noontime, Oliver helped Carrie take the cake and cookies to school. Mrs. Woodfield had wrapped them carefully, and Oliver got all the way to school without dropping any cookies. Carrie, of course, had charge of the cake.

Halfway to school they met Oliver's friend Freddy Miller, who struggled along with a large, old-fashioned combination clock-and-barometer.

"What's *that?*" Carrie balanced her cake plate carefully and looked at Freddy with curiosity.

Freddy was a small, freckle-faced boy, not quite as tall as Oliver, and he was having a hard time with the carrying. But he was proud of his contribution to the auction.

"The winding thing's broken on the clock, but the barometer still works."

"That's nice." Carrie smiled politely. She didn't think many people would want a clock that wouldn't run, but she didn't want to hurt Freddy's feelings.

"What does the barometer do?" Oliver asked with a puzzled expression.

"It tells—well, like when there's going to be a storm," Freddy explained.

Oliver had never heard of anything like that. But sure enough, he could see the words printed around the face of the barometer: STORMY — RAIN — CHANGE — FAIR — DRY.

There was an arrow, pointing now to FAIR.

"It sure is heavy." Freddy shifted the clumsy burden and trailed along behind Oliver with his cookies and Carrie with her cake. Carrie held the cake proudly, gripping the plate firmly with both hands, and when her girl friends came hovering around her in the school yard she said, "Don't bump me!"

They went to the school gymnasium, where tables had been pushed together in a long line. Everybody was there with cakes and pies and cookies and doughnuts. Everything looked so good, Oliver wished he could sample something, but then they had to go up to their classrooms.

Oliver thought the afternoon would never end, he was so eager to get back downstairs to the gym. All the children were restless, but Miss Lee understood and she didn't get cross. She was looking forward to the bake sale and auction, too. She had on a new dress and dangling gold earrings that swung back and forth when she turned her head.

And finally it was three o'clock.

It was time for the bake sale and auction.

Oliver took a chair on the stage at the end of the gym. Everybody who was going to auction a service got to sit on the stage. Oliver picked a chair right in the very front row, and his friend Freddy sat next to him.

At one side of the stage was a long table with the things some of the children and teachers had brought to be sold at the auction: Freddy's clock, and vases, and books. There were also a baby's high chair, a ship in a bottle, and a croquet set with only one mallet missing.

Some of the parents and neighborhood people began to gather around the edge of the stage. Others wandered along beside the display of cakes and pies and cookies and doughnuts. Oliver saw his mother there, and he hoped she would buy a big chocolate cake and bring it home for supper.

"Ladies and gentlemen—your attention, please."

Mr. Kenmore, the science teacher, stood in the middle of the stage. He was a plump, ruddy man, and all the children liked his science lessons. He kept white mice and gerbils and had a cabinet full of rock specimens and seashells. And he had a stuffed owl under a glass dome. His room was very interesting.

"We are now going to start the auction," he said, "so why don't you all move up here a little closer."

Mr. Kenmore waited, and gradually the people who had been standing beside the bakery goods came down the gym toward the stage. A large crowd collected. Oliver was glad to see that Dr. Adams did not seem to be there—Dr. Adams with his big house and yard and half a million trees.

Then Oliver saw the old witch lady standing at the side of the crowd, a pocketbook over one arm, a large black hat on her head. The old witch lady had come to the auction!

Oliver watched her curiously. Why had *she* come?

he wondered. To cast a spell on someone? Anyway, he thought, she wouldn't bid on anything. Everybody said she didn't have any money.

Well, not everybody. Some people said she only *seemed* to be poor, but that she really had pots of money all over her house. Oliver wondered which story was true.

Freddy saw Mrs. Prichard at the same time, and he poked Oliver. "Hey, look who's here."

But Oliver didn't have time to answer. The auction was beginning.

"Joanne Brown." Mr. Kenmore called the first name, and a tall redheaded girl from the seventh grade got up from her chair and walked to the front of the stage to stand beside the science teacher.

"Joanne is going to auction two evenings of baby-sitting," Mr. Kenmore announced, and this time Oliver poked Freddy and whispered, "Can't girls think of anything else to do?"

"Two dollars," a lady in the middle of the crowd called eagerly.

"Two dollars," Mr. Kenmore repeated loudly. "Do I hear more? Do I hear three dollars? Three dollars?"

"Two and a half," another lady called.

"Three dollars." The first lady did not want to lose her baby-sitter.

One by one the children came to the front of the stage as their names were called. Freddy got five dollars for shoveling snow when winter came. Mr. Kenmore's gavel rapped louder and faster on the little table; his face grew ruddier and ruddier. Oliver could hardly wait for his turn, and finally his name was called at last.

"Now here we have a boy who will keep your yard clear of leaves all fall," Mr. Kenmore promised cheerfully. He put his hand on Oliver's shoulder. "What am I bid, ladies and gentlemen?"

"Two dollars," someone called out.

"Three dollars," another called.

"Three dollars." Mr. Kenmore beamed. "Do I hear four? Do I hear four?"

"Four dollars," said a voice from the crowd.

"Four dollars. Do I hear five?" Mr. Kenmore asked. "Do I hear five?"

Mr. Kenmore waited. But no one offered five dollars.

"Four dollars once. Four dollars twice." Mr. Kenmore banged his gavel on the table. "Sold for four dollars to the lady in the black hat."

And from the sea of faces the old witch lady looked straight up at Oliver.

A Black Cat
and Closed-Up Rooms

"The afternoon certainly was a success," Oliver's mother said happily. "The library has a lot of money for new books and things now."

They had come home from the bake sale and auction, and Mrs. Woodfield still had her hat on as she hurried around the kitchen getting supper ready. She was behind schedule because of the auction, and had asked Carrie to help by making a salad. Now Carrie was standing at the sink chopping lettuce and tomatoes.

"But Oliver has to rake leaves for Mrs. Prichard." Carrie wrinkled up her face.

"I won't let her put any spells on *me*," Oliver boasted.

"I don't think she will put any spells on you," his mother said impatiently.

"She will so," Carrie said under her breath.

Oliver thought about the black cat he sometimes saw in Mrs. Prichard's yard. It was a big cat with glowing yellow eyes. Sometimes it was sitting right in the middle of the top front-porch step, like a guard.

"Maybe she really is a witch—she has that big black cat," Oliver reminded his mother.

"Lots of people have black cats," his mother said. "That doesn't make them witches."

"But she only eats tomato soup," Oliver said. Everybody knew that.

"Maybe she likes tomato soup," his mother suggested.

It still seemed strange to Oliver.

"And the kids say she has pots of money all over her house," he persisted.

Mrs. Woodfield was not sure what to say to that. She, too, had heard these rumors, but she had never quite believed them. She began to pour milk into glasses, while she thought of how she could answer Oliver.

"Sure," Carrie said, "I bet she does have pots of money. She had enough money today to get Oliver to

16

rake her leaves, and she even bought that old Freddy's and it doesn't even work."

"That's right, she bought Freddy's clock," Oliver reminded his mother. "Why would she want that?"

"She probably wants to know when storms are coming," Carrie decided. "That's probably when she does her best witch work."

"Now, Carrie," Mrs. Woodfield said with exasperation. "That's enough of that kind of talk."

"And why does she keep all her rooms closed up?" Oliver wanted to know next. "Freddy says there's all kinds of witches' things in all those closed-up rooms."

Mrs. Woodfield frowned to herself. Yes, Mrs. Prichard did have some unexplainable ways. . . . "Oliver, please tell your father that supper is ready." Mrs. Woodfield decided to end the talk about Mrs. Prichard. "And here—put my hat somewhere."

Oliver went into the living room, where his father was reading the evening paper. His father looked calm and happy, Oliver thought. He didn't have to worry about raking leaves for Mrs. Prichard.

That night when Oliver went to bed he thought about the old witch lady putting a spell on him. But maybe he would be safe out in the yard raking leaves.

She couldn't do anything bad to him there, could she? He would be all right if he just didn't go inside her house.

But still he was not very happy, thinking of the old house in the shadows of the myrtle trees, with pale slits of light showing below the pulled-down blinds.

The Creaking Swing

Every afternoon when he walked home from school Oliver looked at Mrs. Prichard's yard. It was early October, and the leaves were beginning to fall.

But every day he thought, No, there aren't enough leaves to rake yet.

Freddy and the other kids were always asking, "Hey, Oliver, when are you going to start raking leaves for the old witch lady?"

"There aren't enough to rake yet," Oliver always said. He walked by Mrs. Prichard's house on his way home from school and stuck his hands in his trouser pockets.

Even Miss Lee, Oliver's teacher, asked him one

day if he had gone over to rake Mrs. Prichard's yard.

"No, I haven't been yet," Oliver said, looking down at his shoes.

School was over for the day, and the other children clattered out, but Oliver lingered by Miss Lee's desk.

"I didn't think I'd ever seen you there," Miss Lee said. "I live right across the street, you know."

Oliver looked up with interest. He hadn't known that Miss Lee lived across the street from the old witch lady.

"Have you ever been inside her house?" Oliver asked curiously.

"No." Miss Lee shook her head. "She keeps pretty much to herself. But sometimes, on summer nights, she sits on her porch in that old swing. It creaks, and if I'm on my porch I can hear it. It sounds rather strange. Not a lamp lit in all the house, or any other sign of activity—just the creak-creak of the swing."

Miss Lee paused a moment, and then added confidingly, "I can never actually see her there in the darkness, with the bushes growing up high at the porch railing. I can just hear the swing creaking, so I know she's there."

Maybe she *isn't*, Oliver thought with a shiver. Maybe she isn't there at all. Maybe it's just the swing

moving by itself. That seemed like something that might happen at a witch's house.

He was glad he didn't live across the street from Mrs. Prichard. He didn't think he'd like to lie in bed at night and listen to creaking sounds from a dark and silent house where he couldn't really *see* anyone in the shadows.

Miss Lee gathered up her purse and some books. She glanced at the schoolroom clock, the way people look at a clock when they have someplace to go and should be on their way.

"I've got to run, Oliver. I have a dentist appointment and I'm afraid I'm late."

Miss Lee started toward the door, and Oliver walked beside her. The corridor beyond was deserted. The other children had already gone, and with a quick "Good-bye" and a click of heels on the stairway, Miss Lee was gone too.

Oliver got his jacket from his locker and pulled it on as he thought about what Miss Lee had said. It was too bad Miss Lee had never been in the old witch lady's house. She could have told Oliver what it was like inside. She might have found out what was in the closed-up rooms.

Oliver walked slowly toward the stairs, zipping his jacket.

Maybe if he went into the house he could find out for himself.

No. He wasn't really sure he wanted to go inside. He was just going to rake leaves in the yard.

He wasn't really sure he even wanted to rake leaves!

Oliver's mother didn't say anything all that week. But as the next week began to pass by and Oliver still did not say anything about starting to rake leaves, his mother said at last, "Oliver, don't you think it's time you got started at Mrs. Prichard's house? I went by there the other day, and her yard has a lot of leaves."

"I didn't see very many," Oliver said.

"You take a better look tomorrow when you come home from school," Mrs. Woodfield suggested. She was sewing a button on one of Oliver's shirts, and the thimble clicked against the needle. "I think you'll see quite a few leaves to be raked if you look hard."

"I looked hard today."

Mrs. Woodfield was silent a moment, drawing the thread through the button. Then she said, "Oliver, it was kind of Mrs. Prichard to try to help the school library. You don't want to disappoint her."

"It was only four dollars," Oliver protested. Carrie had gotten six dollars for two evenings of baby-sitting. Freddy had been promised five dollars for shoveling snow when winter came.

"Nevertheless," his mother continued, "it was kind of Mrs. Prichard to try to help. You know, Oliver, she may *not* have pots of money all over that house. Just because people say she does doesn't make it so."

But maybe it *is* so, Oliver thought. Maybe if he did go inside, he could find out. Maybe he could find out for sure one way or the other, and solve the mystery all the kids talked about.

"Oliver, Mrs. Prichard has paid her money," Mrs. Woodfield said more firmly. "She expects you to rake the leaves. She is probably looking for you every day."

Looking for him every day. Was she hiding behind the curtains at her windows, Oliver wondered, watching especially for *him* as he walked home from school?

He didn't like that idea much. Maybe she'd get mad and put a spell on him if he didn't start raking those leaves soon.

Scary Adventure
on a Dark Night

Oliver hoped he wouldn't meet the old witch lady on the street one day. "Why haven't you come yet to rake my leaves?" she would ask, bending her bony old face down close to his. Oliver didn't think he'd like that.

But when he did see her—well, he did see her and he didn't.

It was Thursday night, and Freddy came by after supper. Although it was already growing dusky, Mrs. Woodfield said Oliver could go uptown with Freddy to the ice-cream shop.

In the summer the ice-cream shop was always crowded, but on this cool October evening Freddy and Oliver were the only customers and they took their time walking up and down the glass case where the ice-cream tubs were sunk in a refrigerated unit. There were so many flavors it was hard to decide. The attendant, in a white apron and cap, waited patiently, lounging back against a rear counter, arms across his chest.

Chocolate-butter-pecan delight.

Raspberry-cherry dream.

Marshmallow swirl.

Finally Freddy had decided to take the chocolate-chip dip and Oliver had chosen the chocolate-chocolate (which was *very* chocolaty). The attendant wrapped a paper napkin around the cones, and the boys went back out to the street, licking the ice cream. It was growing quite dark, and later Oliver wondered if it was because of the dark that he had been mistaken... for he thought he saw Mrs. Prichard coming toward them along the street. Freddy hadn't noticed, and Oliver looked down at his cone, hoping that if he didn't see her, she wouldn't see him. But he knew she was coming straight toward them.

And then when he looked up—she was gone.

The street was deserted, except for two highschool girls walking along, swinging their purses. The street lamps were on, casting pools of silvery light on the pavement, and passing cars had their headlights turned on.

All the stores were closed now, except the ice-cream shop they had just left and a coffee shop across the street. Oliver could see people there, in the booths by the windows, and a cheery red sign flashed off and on: TONY'S DINER - GOOD FOOD DAY AND NIGHT.

But the witch lady was gone . . . if it really had been her!

Oliver turned to tell Freddy, who had dropped behind a few steps to put his paper napkin in a trash container. Paper napkins were only an unnecessary nuisance when he was trying to enjoy an ice-cream cone.

"Freddy—"

But just as he turned, Oliver collided with a tall, stern-looking man who was hurrying along the street. The chocolate-chocolate ice cream cone jammed right into the front of the man's shirt.

The man caught his balance and glared down at Oliver in the fading light. His face was as thin and mean as any face Oliver had ever seen.

"Look what you've done!" The man towered above Oliver. He seemed as tall as the street lamp, which

marked deep shadows on his angry face.

Oliver gasped with fright and embarrassment.

The man looked past Oliver along the street, but even the two girls had passed now and the street was empty.

"Here—" Oliver offered the man his paper napkin, but the man brushed it aside impatiently. Instead he yanked a handkerchief out of his pocket and hurried on into the darkness.

Freddy had stood aside a little, waiting, safely out of the way of the angry man. "Gee, he sure looked mad," he said, as he caught up with Oliver again.

But Oliver had remembered Mrs. Prichard.

"Hey, Freddy. Just now I thought I saw the old witch lady—and then she just disappeared."

"What do you mean, disappeared?" Freddy licked his ice cream and blinked at Oliver.

"She was there, right there." Oliver pointed to the deserted street ahead. "And then, when I looked again, she wasn't there anymore. She just disappeared."

Freddy frowned. "Maybe she went into a store or something."

"There aren't any stores open," Oliver said.

It was true. The boys walked along slowly. One by one, as they passed the stores—MARIE'S FINE

HATS—BONTON CANDIES—WILKES OFFICE SUP-
PLIES—they could see that they were all closed for
the night.

"She probably went down the alley." Freddy
pulled at Oliver's sleeve and pointed down a dimly lit
alley stretching along the side of WILKES OFFICE
SUPPLIES.

They stood at the alley entrance and peered into
the gloom beyond. There was certainly no one there
now. A few empty cardboard packing boxes at the
rear door of the office-supply store were the only
things in sight.

"Why would she go down there?" Oliver said.

Freddy's eyes were solemn in his freckled face.
"Shall we go and see?"

It all seemed very mysterious and witchy to
Oliver. He didn't think he wanted to go down the
dark alley looking for Mrs. Prichard.

Freddy didn't really seem to want to go very much
either. The alley looked long and scary. A silence
hung over it, as though it were a thousand miles away
from the sound of traffic in the street and the cozy
lights of the diner across the way.

And it *was* empty. If Mrs. Prichard had gone
there, she was not there now.

Inside the
Witch Lady's House

There was no putting off the raking any longer. On Saturday morning Oliver put on his blue jeans and sneakers and set off for Mrs. Prichard's house with a rake and a large plastic bag for the leaves.

He didn't meet anyone he knew along the way, until he reached Mrs. Prichard's block. Miss Lee was just pulling her car to the curb in front of her house. She got out and waved across the street to Oliver. Her coat was bright red, and her hair was tied back with a red scarf.

"Going to rake?"

It was more a greeting than a question, for there was Oliver with his rake over his shoulder.

Oliver waved back, and Miss Lee took a bag of groceries from the back seat of her car and went on up the walk to her house. When she closed the door, the street was empty again, except for Oliver and his rake...and the old witch lady's house.

Her front porch had an abandoned look. Several empty flower pots by the doorway seemed a sad reminder that summer was long gone. The porch swing hung motionless.

Oliver went along the side of Mrs. Prichard's house to the backyard, and began to rake the leaves as fast as he could.

He had not raked for more than five minutes when Mrs. Prichard came to her kitchen door and called, "*Boy.*"

Oliver looked around, but there was no one else in sight anywhere. She was calling *him*.

Oliver edged toward the back steps.

Mrs. Prichard stood by the door. She was very thin and bony, and unsmiling, and Oliver walked slower and slower.

"*Boy,*" she called again, in a reedy old voice.

When he came to a stop at the foot of the steps, she stood holding the door open for him to come in. Lagging, Oliver went up the steps. He *wanted* to go inside, but at the same time he *didn't* want to. He wanted to have more time to make up his mind. Unfortunately she held the door wider and he didn't have any more time.

"Come along, come along," she muttered, shaking her head because he walked so slowly.

Oliver opened his mouth to say, "No, thanks," but his mouth was dry inside. He clutched his rake like a weapon and crept through the kitchen door.

The kitchen was dim and gloomy. At the sink a droplet of water formed at the faucet and fell with a sudden quiver. The black cat stared out silently at Oliver from under a kitchen chair, and the floor creaked as Mrs. Prichard walked across it.

"I have something for you."

Oliver watched as she opened a drawer in one of the kitchen cabinets and took out a worn pair of gardening gloves. Beyond the kitchen, through a dark, narrow hallway, Oliver could see the front parlor. He could see a table and a chair and Freddy's old clock from the auction.

Along the hallway were closed doors. Closed-up rooms. And upstairs? Oliver glanced toward the kitchen ceiling. Were there more closed-up rooms upstairs? That was what everybody said. What could be in all the rooms, behind the closed doors...?

"It isn't good to rake leaves without gloves," Mrs.

Prichard was saying. Veins stood out on the side of her forehead. Her nose was long, sharp, bony. "It makes blisters."

She held out the gloves to Oliver.

He could see a can of tomato soup on the shelf by the stove. He didn't see anything else to eat, just a can of tomato soup.

And then he heard the clock that didn't run striking *bong-bong-bong* in the parlor.

The Face
at the Window

Once he was outside again, Oliver began to feel excited. He raked the leaves faster and faster. He had been inside the old witch lady's house! None of the other kids ever had!

And he could tell everyone it was true: the old witch lady ate only tomato soup. And he had seen lots of closed doors.

And he had heard the clock strike.

When Oliver had finished raking, he left the gloves beside the back door and tiptoed down the steps. Behind him the house was quiet, and he wondered if Mrs. Prichard was watching him leave. He couldn't tell.

Just as Oliver reached the sidewalk in front of Mrs. Prichard's front yard, he saw the tall, stern-looking man again—the one he had collided with on the street by the ice-cream shop—and he was bearing down on Oliver at full steam. Then, when Oliver was beginning to wonder where he could hide, the man swept by without even a glance at him and hurried up the walk to Mrs. Prichard's house.

Oliver drew a sigh of relief. Either the man was just in too much of a hurry to notice him, or he hadn't recognized him. If the man had recognized him, Oliver thought he would probably get angry and say, "Aren't you the boy who got ice cream all over me?"

The man rang Mrs. Prichard's doorbell, and then began to pound on her front door. *Pound* was the only way to describe it. It was much too loud and fierce to be called knocking.

Oliver had started to go on, but his steps slowed and he kept looking over his shoulder. He had never heard anyone bang so hard on a door. Mrs. Prichard would probably trip over her black cat rushing to see what all the commotion was.

But Mrs. Prichard did not appear at all.

The pounding continued, and the door remained unopened.

Oliver stopped then, watching curiously. Mrs.

Prichard was home. She had given him the gardening gloves. Why didn't she come to the door?

Well, maybe she had gone out after she gave him the gloves. She could have gone through the front yard, and Oliver wouldn't have seen her go as he raked in the back. That was it, he decided.

Oliver was about to start on, the better to be safely out of the way whenever the man tired of pounding at the door and came back to the sidewalk, but again his steps slowed. At an upstairs window he saw a curtain move, drawn aside just a few inches by a hand. It was hard to tell, but Oliver thought he saw a glimpse of a face, and then as the curtain remained parted, he was sure. Someone was standing there by the upstairs window watching.

It gave Oliver a very eerie feeling. Someone was watching the yard below. Someone was listening to the racket at the door and not answering, just waiting.

Finally the noise stopped. The tall man turned and stood uncertainly at the top of the porch steps a moment. Then, with an angry gesture, he came down the steps and walked toward the sidewalk.

Oliver thought he had lingered long enough and he hurried on, but not before he saw that the face at the upstairs window had withdrawn, the hand had

disappeared, and the curtain had fallen back into place.

The man walked off in the opposite direction from Oliver, so there was nothing to worry about after all.

Oliver went on, his rake over his shoulder. He was glad to get away from the old witch lady's house and that silent face at the window.

All the same, it *was* going to be great telling Freddy and the other kids that he had really, truly been *inside*.

Oliver didn't have to wait long for his chance. Halfway home he met Freddy and a gang of neighborhood children kicking an empty tin can along the sidewalk. They could tell by the rake over Oliver's shoulder where *he* had been.

"Did you really go and rake the old witch lady's leaves?" Freddy asked right away. His freckled face was bright with interest.

The boys and girls clustered around Oliver eagerly, forgetting whose turn it was to kick the can, now that Oliver had come walking by with his rake.

"Sure," Oliver said boldly. "I was even inside her house."

"You *were!*"

"Sure," Oliver said. "I went right inside. I'm not afraid."

"Did you see any pots of money?" one of the boys wanted to know.

"No," Oliver admitted. "But I saw the tomato soup and a lot of closed-up doors." He was going to add that he had heard the clock striking, but another of the boys interrupted.

"What do you suppose she has hidden in those closed-up rooms?"

Someone else said, "I bet that's where all her money is."

"Naw," Freddy argued, "that's where she keeps all her witch stuff for mixing up things and casting spells."

"You better not go in again, Oliver," one of the girls warned. "Maybe next time you won't get out."

But Oliver had been in the old witch lady's house once, and he had escaped safely. He could do it again. He had seen the tomato-soup can and the closed doors—but that wasn't enough. He had to find out what was in those rooms.

Pots of money?

Or things for witches' spells?

And how could a clock that didn't work strike *bong-bong-bong*? He could still hear its echo in his mind.

Mrs. Adams'
Mysterious Story

When Oliver got home with his rake, Dr. Adams' wife was sitting in the kitchen visiting with Oliver's mother. They were drinking coffee, and Mrs. Adams' bracelets jingled on her arm every time she raised her cup.

She was a small woman with soft, wavy black hair and a friendly smile. Her coat and handbag were beside her on an empty chair.

"Hello, Oliver," she said. "You look as though you've been working hard."

"Oliver has been raking leaves for Mrs. Prichard," Oliver's mother explained.

"Is that so?" Mrs. Adams made a funny face. "She

certainly is a queer one, isn't she?"

Before Mrs. Woodfield could say anything, Oliver blurted out, "I went in her house—and I saw the tomato soup—and I heard the clock."

"What clock?" Mrs. Adams had not been at the school auction.

"How did you happen to be in the house, Oliver?" Mrs. Woodfield asked.

"She wanted to give me a pair of gloves so I wouldn't get blisters."

"That was thoughtful of her," Oliver's mother said.

"And I saw the rooms all closed up." Oliver paused. "It was sort of spooky."

Mrs. Woodfield laughed. "Nonsense. Now you better get cleaned up. It's nearly time for lunch."

When Oliver had gone upstairs, Mrs. Adams leaned toward Mrs. Woodfield and lowered her voice confidingly. "I guess she didn't disappear while Oliver was there."

"What do you mean?" Mrs. Woodfield looked at her friend with sudden renewed interest.

Mrs. Adams leaned back in her chair and shook her head. Bracelets glittered on her arm. "I never will forget the afternoon Mrs. Bemis and I were there. It was the strangest thing."

"What happened?" Oliver's mother was very curious now.

"Well, there we were," Mrs. Adams said with a puzzled expression, "sitting in her parlor. It's such a queer, old-fashioned house you feel you've gone back through a time machine.

"Anyway, there we were, Mrs. Bemis and I, and Mrs. Prichard said she thought she'd get a shawl. She went into a side parlor and closed the door. We waited a few minutes, but she didn't come back.

"After a while I got up and rapped on the door to the side parlor, and I called, 'Mrs. Prichard?' But there was no answer."

"No answer?" Mrs. Woodfield repeated.

"No answer." Mrs. Adams paused dramatically. "Mrs. Bemis and I waited a few more minutes. We thought maybe there was a stairway in that side parlor, and Mrs. Prichard had gone upstairs for her shawl.

"But finally a good deal of time passed, and we didn't want to wait any longer. So I opened the door and looked in. *And Mrs. Prichard wasn't there!*"

Mrs. Woodfield looked at Mrs. Adams blankly, and Mrs. Adams repeated: "Mrs. Prichard just wasn't there."

Mrs. Woodfield looked at Mrs. Adams in silence.

Finally she said, "But she must have been there *some*place."

"No, she wasn't." Mrs. Adams shook her head firmly. "She was not *there*. There wasn't anything there. Not a rug or a stick of furniture, except an old rocker in one corner. It was just an empty room. There wasn't a stairway leading upstairs, or any other door to the room. The curtains were drawn and the room was shadowy, but we could see enough to tell she wasn't there."

"Maybe she was behind the curtains," Mrs. Woodfield suggested. "Oliver hides behind curtains sometimes, to tease Carrie."

But Mrs. Adams was shaking her head again. "No, she wasn't. The curtains were short. They reached only to the windowsill, not to the floor. Nobody could stand behind them. No, she had simply gone into that room and *vanished*."

Mrs. Adams smiled faintly. "Mrs. Bemis said afterward that maybe Mrs. Prichard sat down in that rocker and said some magic words and disappeared."

"What did you do then?" Oliver's mother asked. Her coffee had grown cold while she listened to Mrs. Adams' story.

"What was there to do?" Mrs. Adams said. "There we were, Mrs. Bemis and I, completely alone in that eerie old house. I tell you, we didn't stay a moment longer. We put on our gloves and let ourselves out the front door. And we've never gone back since."

"It must have been a strange experience," Mrs. Woodfield said thoughtfully.

"Strange isn't the word for it." Mrs. Adams had finished her coffee, and she reached for her coat. "It was downright scary, that's what it was."

When Oliver came downstairs, Mrs. Adams had gone. Mrs. Woodfield had rinsed the coffee cups and gone down into the basement. Oliver could hear the washing machine.

Lunch didn't seem to be ready, so Oliver got some cookies from the cookie jar and sat down at the kitchen table. It was nice to be in his own cheery kitchen. Mrs. Prichard's kitchen had been dim and creepy. The black cat had stared at him and the floor had creaked as Mrs. Prichard came toward him with the gloves.

But it was kind of her to give him the gloves, wasn't it? Maybe she wasn't really a witch.

Still, he had heard the clock. And he had seen that long dark hallway with all the closed-up rooms.

Poisoned Cake?

The next Saturday it looked like rain, but Oliver set out again for Mrs. Prichard's house. He carried his rake and, this time, he took along a pair of his mother's gardening gloves. Mrs. Prichard would have no excuse to call him in now.

But he had only been raking a few minutes when the kitchen door opened again. *"Boy."*

The call floated in the chill October wind across the gray and leaf-strewn yard.

Oliver looked toward the house. There stood the old witch lady, just as she had stood before, holding the door open for him to come in. Her black dress came nearly to her ankles, and the cat crouched at her feet.

She beckoned to him with a wrinkled, bony hand,

and this time she stepped away from the door, back into the kitchen, where Oliver couldn't see her anymore.

Oliver took a few steps toward the house, then waited a moment at the foot of the porch steps. He could see the open kitchen door, but in the dimness beyond that he could not see anything.

At last he went up a step or two, and finally he went up all the way.

Across the room, Mrs. Prichard stood beside a small table. A candle was burning on the table. *A candle in the daytime . . . ?* But before Oliver could think any more about that, Mrs. Prichard had turned toward him and he saw a large knife glittering in her hand.

"Come in, boy."

Oliver did not move.

Was she going to cut him up into pieces with that knife? Or slit him in two? His heart began to pound. It wasn't worth *that* just to tell Freddy and the other kids that he'd been inside the old witch lady's house again.

Candlelight flickered on the knife blade.

"What's the matter?" Her voice was raspy, and the black cat sprang up onto the table beside the candle and arched its back.

"My—my shoes are dirty," Oliver stammered.

"Heh, heh, heh." Her laugh sounded just like a witch's laugh. She looked at Oliver a moment longer, and then she put down the knife and took something from the table.

"I thought you might like a piece of cake."

Oliver shook his head, but she came steadily toward him, holding out the piece of cake.

"I'm not hungry."

"Boys are always hungry."

The way the light fell on her spectacles Oliver could not see her eyes. It gave her a spooky look.

She forced the cake into his hand.

Oliver backed away, clutching the piece of cake so tightly he would have crumbled it to bits except that it was a strangely hard piece of cake, not like the soft cakes his mother made. Something was *wrong* with it.

Oliver went down the steps and glanced back over his shoulder. Mrs. Prichard stood at the kitchen door with the wind ruffling the skirt of her long dress and the black cat rubbing against her ankle.

Oliver tried to smile, but his mouth felt stiff. He thought that when Mrs. Prichard wasn't looking, he would throw the cake into the pile of leaves he was raking, but she kept standing at the kitchen door watching and waiting.

At last he took a few bites of the cake. It was dry and hard, and the frosting cracked off and fell to the ground.

Mrs. Prichard was still watching.

Oliver crammed the rest of the cake into his mouth. It was probably poisoned cake, he thought with panic. He would die a slow, painful death, gasping for breath and falling down at last on the cold ground while Mrs. Prichard watched from her doorway.

Mrs. Prichard was still watching at the door, and Oliver began to rake as fast as he could. Maybe he could get home before he died from the poisoned cake.

"That was kind of Mrs. Prichard to give you some cake," Oliver's mother said.

"But it was funny hard cake—" Oliver started to say, and Carrie, who was sitting at the kitchen table threading a needle (she was learning how to sew), nodded and said, "Ugh, I bet it was, if the old witch lady gave it to you."

"*Carrie.*" Mrs. Woodfield said with great exasperation.

"I mean Mrs. Prichard," Carrie corrected herself with a sigh. She licked the thread and frowned at the needle. She was not sure whether or not she was going to like sewing.

Oliver went to bed that night without feeling any bad effects from eating Mrs. Prichard's queer cake.

There was no wind, and the blue curtains at his window hung motionless. In the darkness he could just make out the shape of his bureau across the room.

A siren sounded briefly, far off, and then the night was silent again.

Oliver woke to bright sunshine the next morning, not poisoned or dying at all. . . . Yet there were a lot of strange things about old Mrs. Prichard and her house.

Did she have pots of money or not?

Could he find out what was in all those closed-up rooms?

Could he find out why the clock was striking?

Poisoned Lemonade?

The next Saturday Oliver thought it would be the last time he would have to go to Mrs. Prichard's house. Nearly all the leaves had fallen from the skimpy little trees in her yard. He looked up at the thin black branches. Only a few leaves still clung, fluttering feebly in the wind.

He was finished, he thought. But then how could he get inside her house again to solve all the mysteries?

Did he really want to go in again? He wasn't sure.

Oliver raked as slowly as he could, but Mrs. Prichard did not call to him. Finally he stuffed the leaves into the plastic bag and set it in the alley.

He went back through the yard and along the side of the house toward the street. Even then he thought she might open the kitchen door and call to him. But the house was quiet.

He reached the front yard and was halfway to the street beyond, when suddenly the front door opened.

"*Boy.*"

Oliver stopped still.

"*Boy.*" The call came again, louder and more commanding.

Oliver turned around. There stood Mrs. Prichard at her front door. She was beckoning to him, just as she had done from her kitchen door.

Oliver went toward the rickety front porch. Paint was flaking from the steps... and the black cat lay along the top railing, watching Oliver.

"I have something for you," Mrs. Prichard said.

Oliver looked up the steps doubtfully. Now that she had actually called him he wasn't so sure he wanted to go into her house again, after all. And yet, if he did, maybe he would see the pots of money. They weren't in the kitchen, but maybe they were somewhere in the front rooms of her house. This might be his only chance to find out.

Oliver laid his rake against the bottom porch step.

Should I go in, or shouldn't I? he was thinking to himself as he climbed the stairs slowly. Something brushed against his leg, and he saw the black cat slithering past him into the house.

Oliver stood in a small entryway. The pendulum of a large grandfather clock glinted in the light. Beyond lay Mrs. Prichard's living room, but he didn't see any pots of money. It was a creaky old room with old-fashioned chairs and faded lace curtains at the windows. An ancient piano with yellowing keys stood against one wall, and several clocks on the mantel ticked loudly in the silence.

In fact, there were a lot of clocks....

Suddenly Oliver wanted to run. But it was too late. He could not get out now. Mrs. Prichard had closed the door behind him, and she was standing between him and the door.

"I've made you some lemonade." She bent down and put her withered old face close to his. Tendrils of gray hair poked from behind her ears.

For a moment Oliver stared into the eyes behind the spectacles, in the old face so close to his. He didn't want any lemonade, but when he didn't move, Mrs. Prichard took hold of his shoulder with her scrawny hand and drew him along into the parlor toward a chair.

"Sit here," she said in her raspy voice. "It's all ready."

Oliver sat down on the edge of a chair, and Mrs. Prichard sat down on the sofa. The black cat jumped up beside her and lay on a sofa cushion, staring at Oliver with an unblinking gaze.

On a small table by the sofa there was a tray with a glass of lemonade and a cup and saucer, a teapot, and a bowl of sugar. Mrs. Prichard handed the glass to Oliver.

"I made tea for myself."

Oliver's hands were so shaky he had to hold the glass with both hands. Why wasn't she having lemonade, too? Was there poison in the lemonade? Or a witch's brew to put a spell on him?

Mrs. Prichard was watching him with a peculiar smile, one thin finger tapping the arm of the sofa. The afternoon had grown dark, but only one lamp was lighted. Behind Mrs. Prichard a long shadow rose upon the wall in the room full of clocks.

"Do you like my house?"

Her voice startled Oliver and he almost dropped the lemonade.

"Everything's old now." Her spectacles glistened in the light. "Old like me. Heh, heh, heh." She laughed an eerie, high-pitched laugh, and Oliver felt

sure any moment she was going to spring at him and snatch him with her skeleton fingers.

But then the raspy laugh died away.

"More sugar?"

She lifted the sugar bowl and held it out toward Oliver.

"Go on, help yourself." She held the sugar closer to Oliver. "I don't use sugar myself."

Oliver stared at the sugar bowl. Maybe the poison was in the sugar!

"No—no, thank you." Oliver shook his head.

He wasn't going to take any of that sugar. And he wasn't going to drink any of that lemonade.

"Drink your lemonade," Mrs. Prichard ordered, as though she had read his mind. The sugar bowl clinked back on the tray.

Oliver sat a little closer to the edge of the chair. His fingers felt numb from holding the cold glass so tightly. Maybe he could take just one little sip, he thought.

But no, maybe even one little sip would be enough to poison him—or to change him into a toad or a bat.

"I collect clocks," Mrs. Prichard said, and then at just that moment Oliver heard the same *bong-bong-bong* he had heard before. Only it wasn't Freddy's clock, which didn't work after all. It was one of the clocks on a cabinet by the window.

"I have sixteen, if you count the whole house." Mrs. Prichard motioned to include other rooms. "But they don't all work. Heh, heh, heh."

She seemed to find this quite amusing, and it was a moment before her cackling laughter faded.

When she grew quiet again, Oliver did not know what to say. He wished he were home.

A sudden, sharp ring of the doorbell broke in upon the silence of the room. Almost at once, as though whoever was there could not wait for the bell to be answered, a loud sound of knocking and pounding began on the door.

Mrs. Prichard did not move, as though she hoped whoever was knocking would go away if she didn't answer. But the knocking only grew louder.

Oliver couldn't help peeking over his shoulder at the door, and at last Mrs. Prichard said with annoyance, "Now who can that be?"

Oliver was sure *he* knew who it was, even if Mrs. Prichard didn't. The man he had seen pounding on the door before had come back again. He had come to see Mrs. Prichard—and now he would find Oliver there, the boy who had almost knocked him down and jammed ice cream all over his shirt.

Mrs. Prichard put her teacup on the table and

stood up with a sigh. Oliver remembered how before, when the man came, she had only watched at the window, not answering the door. He had a feeling she wouldn't have answered this time either, if she'd been alone. But Oliver was there. He wanted to say, "It's all right with *me* if you don't answer."

The pounding on the door continued, and Oliver watched as Mrs. Prichard went into the entryway and opened the door.

The Stranger
Comes Back

The tall, thin man stood on the porch, outlined queerly against the pale light of the October sky.

"Oh," Mrs. Prichard said. "It's *you!*"

"Yes, it's me."

The man came in, brushing past Mrs. Prichard and stopping with a frown when he saw Oliver. He had thought Mrs. Prichard was alone.

"This boy has been raking my leaves." Mrs. Prichard closed the door and came back into the parlor. Her mouth had a tight, pinched look.

The man looked at Oliver, at first with vague recognition, and then he remembered.

"We've met," he said darkly, but then, to Oliver's relief, he turned away without further interest.

Oliver stood up. Maybe now was his chance to escape without drinking the lemonade.

But no such luck.

"Sit down, boy," Mrs. Prichard said. "Finish your lemonade." She passed the man and sat down again by the table.

The man looked at Oliver impatiently. He wanted to talk to Mrs. Prichard alone, Oliver could tell. He didn't want Oliver there.

"This is my cousin, Mr. Harlin," Mrs. Prichard said to Oliver.

"Hello." It was all Oliver could think of to say. He sat down again helplessly on the edge of the sunken old chair.

Mr. Harlin stood with his back to the mantel and the clocks, and frowned at Oliver.

"Sit down," Mrs. Prichard said to him.

"I can conduct my business just as well standing," Mr. Harlin replied firmly.

Oliver peeked at Mr. Harlin. He was glowering at Mrs. Prichard.

"It's chilly in here," Mrs. Prichard said abruptly. "I think I'll just get a shawl."

She got up and went to the door at the side of the parlor.

"I won't be a minute," she said, as she went through and closed the door behind her.

The Witch Lady
Disappears

The house was silent.

Oliver sat on the edge of the chair and held his glass of lemonade. Mr. Harlin stood by the mantel without saying a word. The clocks on the mantel ticked on in the silence. And the black cat stared with yellow eyes.

"I don't have all day," Mr. Harlin exclaimed at last. He walked over to the side parlor door and opened it crossly.

"I don't have all day," he repeated to the room beyond. "I have other things to attend to...."

He stopped speaking, and stood for a moment in the doorway as though surprised at something. Then he walked into the side parlor, leaving the door open behind him. From his chair Oliver could not see much, and he was craning his neck to try to see into the side parlor when suddenly Mr. Harlin called to him.

"Now will you come and explain this to me!"

Oliver got up and went to the side-parlor door. The room beyond was dusky. Curtains were drawn tightly at two small windows. He could see Mr. Harlin standing in the middle of the room, and he could see a rocking chair in one corner of the room. But there was nothing else. Mrs. Prichard was certainly not there.

"Will you just explain this to me," Mr. Harlin demanded again. But he didn't really expect Oliver to answer, and he came striding out of the side parlor, brushing past Oliver and almost spilling his lemonade.

"That woman..." Mr. Harlin was muttering to himself and, to Oliver's surprise, he began to walk along the hallway toward the kitchen, opening all the closed doors as he went along. He stuck his head into each room and looked around angrily.

Oliver followed close behind. Here was his chance to see if there were pots of money or witches' things, and he didn't want to miss it.

The house had three rooms downstairs, and the first two were bare and empty. Curtains were drawn at the windows, but there were no rugs on the floors, no furniture. The third room was scantily furnished with a bed and dresser. No pots of money could be seen in any of the rooms. No witches' brews. And no Mrs. Prichard.

"Where can she have gone?" Mr. Harlin turned and glared at Oliver.

Oliver stared back, and Mr. Harlin turned away with a gesture of irritation. Then he stamped up the stairs at the end of the hall.

Oliver looked up the stairs uncertainly. But he wanted to see what was up there, too, so at last he followed along after Mr. Harlin.

Upstairs there were only two doorways. Mr. Harlin opened both doors and peered into the rooms. Oliver looked in, too. It was the same as downstairs, except that here and there was an old piece of furniture: a lamp, a table, an empty bookcase. But no pots of money. No sign of jars and bottles that would hold witches' potions.

And no Mrs. Prichard.

The upstairs was cold, and Oliver began to shiver. There were no witches' things, but Mrs. Prichard *had* disappeared. Only witches could make themselves disappear, Oliver thought. Not real people.

"Where she has got to I can't imagine," Mr. Harlin announced finally. He shut the doors impatiently. "I have had just about enough of this nonsense."

Mr. Harlin went downstairs again. He seized his

hat from the parlor mantel, and before Oliver could say a word, the tall, angry man opened the front door and walked out, slamming the door behind him.

Oliver stood at the foot of the stairs and blinked at the front door. He thought he should go too, but he still had the glass of lemonade in his hand. He went into the parlor to put the glass back on the table by Mrs. Prichard's teacup. It seemed odd to see her teacup sitting there. Only a few minutes ago she had been holding it, sipping her tea, casting a shadow on the wall.

Oliver set down his glass. On the sofa cushion the black cat watched from its glittering yellow eyes. A clock on the mantel began to strike, *ting—ting—ting*. It was the only sound in all the house.

Oliver was all alone now in the old witch lady's house.

He began to back away toward the front hall, and then, just in case the old witch lady had made herself invisible and was really right there with him even though he couldn't see her, Oliver said, "Well... good-bye..."

"You aren't leaving already, are you? You haven't finished your lemonade."

And there stood Mrs. Prichard in the side-parlor doorway, watching him from behind her spectacles.

The Secret
of the Empty Room

"Now that Mr. Harlin is gone we can finish our tea and lemonade," Mrs. Prichard said.

She sat down on the sofa again, and the black cat flicked its tail.

"Bah, it's gone cold." Mrs. Prichard lifted the teapot and poured fresh tea into her cup. "Why are you standing there, boy? Sit down."

But Oliver could only stare. "Where did you go?" he managed to ask after a moment.

"Where did I go? Why, I only went to get my shawl."

Oliver came a step closer.

"But we looked." He glanced at the side-parlor

door. Mrs. Prichard had closed it again, and the empty room with the rocking chair and curtained windows was shut off from view.

"You did? You looked for me?"

Oliver could not tell whether Mrs. Prichard was angry or only surprised.

"Where did you look?"

"In there—everywhere."

"In there? Heh, heh, heh." Mrs. Prichard began to laugh. Her eyes glinted. Then she leaned toward Oliver. "Would you like to know where I went?"

Oliver nodded. He couldn't take his eyes from the old lady's face.

Mrs. Prichard set down her teacup. "Follow me."

She opened the side-parlor door again, and when Oliver hung back she said, "Come along, boy, if you want to know."

Of course he wanted to know... or did he? Maybe she was going to vanish again and take him with her. Maybe she would make him invisible and he wouldn't know how to become visible again.

But step by step Oliver went across the carpet toward the side-parlor door.

Mrs. Prichard stepped into the side parlor. "Years ago, when my grandfather built this house, he put in a secret door, right here in this room. He did a very good job. No one can tell where it is."

Oliver looked around curiously. He didn't see where a secret door might be.

Mrs. Prichard put her head to one side and watched him. "Can't find it, can you? Nobody can."

Oliver shook his head.

Mrs. Prichard went to one side of the room and pressed her fingers to a certain place on the wall. A panel in the wall opened silently, just like a narrow sliding door.

"Come and see," she said.

When Oliver looked through the doorway he could see a flight of steps leading downward.

"Those steps lead into the cellar," Mrs. Prichard explained. She folded her arms and nodded with satisfaction. "Into the cellar," she repeated.

"Were you in the cellar all the time?" Oliver looked down into the darkness below.

Mrs. Prichard nodded. "There's a window in the cellar. I watched the front walk and I saw Mr. Harlin go. Good riddance, I said to myself. Then I knew it was all right to come up again."

Mrs. Prichard pushed the panel in the wall again, and Oliver heard something click softly back into place. The secret door was closed. It was as though it had never been there.

"Mr. Harlin is my cousin." Mrs. Prichard folded her arms and sighed. "He's a hard man with his money. Stingy, stingy, stingy. I had to borrow some money from him to pay my taxes a few months ago, and I've been trying to pay him back little by little. But he gets impatient, comes banging at the door the way he did today. I didn't have any money to give him just now, so I thought I'd go down into the cellar until he went away."

"Oh." Oliver had never heard of anyone hiding in the cellar until someone went away. But it didn't seem like a bad idea—especially with someone as cross and fierce as Mr. Harlin.

And imagine having a secret door! Oliver looked at Mrs. Prichard with admiration.

"I saw him uptown one night not long ago, and I gave him the slip down an alley. Heh, heh, heh." Wrinkles stretched and deepened as Mrs. Prichard laughed. "I bet he was surprised when I just vanished from the street."

Mr. Harlin wasn't the only one who was surprised, Oliver thought, remembering that strange night very well himself.

"Next week he'll come again," Mrs. Prichard said with assurance. "I'll have some money to give him then, from my pension check. I just didn't want to listen to his fuss today."

Oliver thought that sounded reasonable. Mr. Harlin sure could make a fuss.

"Do you do that a lot?" Oliver asked. "Go down in the cellar?"

"Oh—sometimes," Mrs. Prichard answered vaguely. "Let me see. . . . It wasn't too long ago. Dr. Adams' wife was here with another lady. They had come to collect money for flowers for Mr. Anderson down the street. He died, you know. I didn't have a penny to spare then, but I didn't want to say so."

Mrs. Prichard drew herself up a little straighter and smoothed the front of her dress. She was silent a moment.

"I suppose you noticed that most of the furniture is gone from the rooms. I've sold it bit by bit through the years. I didn't really need it, living by myself, and the extra money helped. I close up the rooms now, and I don't have to heat them in cold weather. That saves money, too."

Oliver felt a sense of excitement to have solved the mystery of Mrs. Prichard's disappearance, and the secret of her closed-up rooms. He had solved a mystery all the kids had wondered about.

And he knew for sure now that she wasn't a witch, even if she did have a house with a secret door. Witches didn't have to hide in cellars.

He could hardly wait to tell Freddy.

"Then you don't really have pots of money?" he asked, looking up at her worn old face and the light shining on her spectacles.

"Heh, heh, heh," she began to laugh. "The only pots I have are in my kitchen."

Oliver Has an Idea

"And those pots probably don't have much in them but tomato soup some days," Oliver's mother said.

She said this when Oliver told her that the only pots Mrs. Prichard had were in her kitchen.

"Isn't that sad," Carrie said softly.

"Yes, it is," Mrs. Woodfield agreed. The newspaper she had put down to talk with Oliver and Carrie rustled softly on her lap. "All the neighborhood children calling her the old witch lady, and there she is just minding her own business and struggling to live on her little bit of money."

"But she gave money at the auction," Oliver said. He was sitting cross-legged on the livingroom floor, still wearing the blue jeans and sweater he had worn that morning to rake the last leaves.

"That just proves she isn't stingy," Carrie said quickly. "She wanted to help the school, and add to her clock collection." She snuggled her feet under her on the couch. Lamplight shone on her silky hair.

Outside in the dark October afternoon the first drops of rain began to fall silently against the windowpanes.

"I'd like to see that clock collection," Carrie mused. "All those clocks that strike at different times, and some that don't even run, like Freddy's with the barometer. He sure had a hard time lugging that to school." She shook her head at the memory.

"I bet that arrow is pointing to rain now." Oliver wished he could see it for himself. Someday he'd like to have a barometer so he could see when the storms were coming.

"I'm sure Mrs. Prichard would be happy to have you see her collection," Mrs. Woodfield said to Carrie. "Most people who have collections like to show them to people. Oliver could take you sometime. She was always kind to Oliver, giving him gloves so he wouldn't get blisters, giving him cake, making him lemonade."

Oliver didn't think it was the time to mention

again how hard and stale the cake had been. In fact, now that he thought back about it, the cake hadn't really been all that bad. The frosting had been a little hard, that was all.

"Half the people around here have always thought Mrs. Prichard was just too stingy to spend money," Mrs. Woodfield said, "and that she really had a lot and was hoarding it. And some people stayed away from her because they thought she was peculiar. I imagine she has had a rather lonely life, besides not having much money."

"We could leave bundles at her door," Carrie began with great excitement. "You know, cans of food and loaves of bread." Her eyes were shining.

Mrs. Woodfield smiled gently. "I don't know how she'd feel about that, Carrie. Sometimes people don't like to accept outright charity."

Carrie looked a little crestfallen. "Well, I could bake her a cake sometimes, couldn't I? That isn't charity."

"I'm sure she'd like that." Mrs. Woodfield smiled gently.

Oliver thought of something *he* could do for Mrs. Prichard. He thought of it all by himself while he was lying in bed that night.

Her house didn't seem scary anymore, now that he knew why the rooms were closed up and how she disappeared and why she ate so much tomato soup. Even her black cat didn't seem spooky anymore. In fact, Oliver rather liked Mrs. Prichard's house, with the little crocheted doilies on the arms of the chairs, the clocks ticking away everywhere, and the room with the secret door. It was really a pretty nice house.

The next morning before he went to school, Oliver wrote a note to Mrs. Prichard, and he left it in her mailbox on his way to school.

It said:

Mrs. Prichard,
  I will shovel your walk when it snows.

                    Oliver Woodfield